The ANGEL & the DONKEY

Retold by

KATHERINE PATERSON

Illustrated by **Alexander Koshkin**

CLARION BOOKS ❧ New York

Clarion Books
a Houghton Mifflin Company imprint
215 Park Avenue South, New York, NY 10003
Text copyright © 1996 by Minna Murra, Inc.
Illustrations copyright © 1996 by Alexander Koshkin

The illustrations for this book were executed in watercolor, tempera, and gouache
onWaterman paper manufactured in Russia.
The text is set in 18/22-point Centaur.

Printed in the USA

For information about this and other Houghton Mifflin trade and reference books and multimedia products,
visit The Bookstore at Houghton Mifflin on the World Wide Web at
(http://www.hmco.com/trade/).

Library of Congress Cataloging-in-Publication Data

Paterson, Katherine.
The angel and the donkey / retold by Katherine Paterson ; illustrated by Alexander Koshkin.
p.   cm.
Summary: A soothsayer and his faithful donkey save the Israelites
from destruction by King Balak on the orders of an angel.
ISBN 0-395-68969-4
1. Balaam (Biblical figure)—Juvenile fiction.   [1. Balaam (Biblical figure)—Fiction.
2. Donkeys—Fiction.]   I. Koshkin, Alexander, ill.   II. Title.
PZ7.P273A1   1996
[Fic]—dc20   94-22430
CIP
AC

HOR 10 9 8 7 6 5 4 3 2 1

For all the angels in my path,
especially Jean Little and Claire Mackay
—K.P.

For Maria Katkova
—A.K.

Thousands of years ago near the river Euphrates in the city of Pethor, there lived a proud and powerful soothsayer named Balaam. Whenever anyone wanted good fortune for himself, or ill fortune for an enemy, he would send for Balaam, and Balaam would come on his faithful donkey and say the proper blessing, or the proper curse, for, of course, the proper fee.

Now it happened that Balak, king of Moab, had a terrible problem. Balak was a fierce and terrible king indeed; his very name meant "to lay waste." But close to Nebo, his capital city, almost in sight of the palace itself, there was an enormous encampment. Balak's spies told him that this multitude of people had been slaves in Egypt. Now, led by a man named Moses, the Israelites (as they called themselves) were looking for a homeland.

Moses had asked Balak's neighbor, Sihon, the king of the Amorites, to give the Israelites safe passage through his territory. King Sihon refused and attacked them instead. But the Israelites fought back. They killed the king, defeated his army, and took over his land.

Balak was alarmed. The people he had thought of as a bunch of puny slaves now loomed as a powerful enemy.

"Why, there are millions of those wretched people!" he cried. "If they march across my county, they'll lick it clean the way a cow clears grass from a field. How can my small army stop them?"

It was then that he remembered Balaam. He gathered some of the elders of the people and ordered them to fetch the soothsayer.

"Tell Balaam to get on that donkey of his and come here immediately," ordered the king. "Tell him I've got an enemy camped here so numerous they cover the ground like a killing frost. I want him to curse them with one of his powerful curses, so that my army will defeat them." For everyone believed Balaam was such a powerful soothsayer that whomever he blessed was blessed indeed, and whomever he cursed was truly cursed.

Balaam was very pleased when the elders of Moab brought him the king's message. He started to get on his donkey then and there, but he didn't want to seem too hasty. Powerful soothsayers should never appear too eager.

"I'd better sleep on it," he said to the elders. "I'll give you my answer in the morning."

That night while Balaam was asleep, dreaming of the huge fee he could demand from the king of Moab, a strange shining creature interrupted his dream.

"Balaam!" the angel said. "Do not go to Moab with Balak's elders."

"Who are you?" Balaam asked, trying not to sound as frightened as he felt.

"I am the messenger of the Lord—the God of those Israelites Balak wants you to curse. You must not curse them, for the Lord has blessed them."

The next morning Balaam told the elders to go back and tell King Balak that he could not come to Moab.

The elders begged him to reconsider, but Balaam, remembering the vision of the angel, said, "Never will I come. Not even if the king were to give me a house piled full of gold and silver."

When Balak heard that Balaam had refused to come, he was angry, but he was also desperate. He knew how proud Balaam was. This time, the king of Moab sent a delegation of his highest officials.

"Tell Balaam that the reward will be beyond his fondest dreams, if only he will come and curse these miserable people for me," the king said.

So the king's officials traveled up to the city of Pethor and delivered the king's message. But the vision of that shining messenger was still fresh in Balaam's mind. He didn't like the idea of crossing the Israelites' God.

"No," said Balaam, "there's no use asking me. As I told your elders, even if the king were to give me a house piled full of silver and gold, I wouldn't disobey the God of Israel."

Not even for a house piled full of gold and silver?

The soothsayer was dazzled by his own words. The Israelites meant nothing to him, but gold and silver . . .

"Perhaps," said Balaam, "I should sleep on it."

That night Balaam tossed and turned. Surely the Israelite God wouldn't object if he went to Moab just to look the situation over. He might be able to work things out happily for everybody. Besides, it would be a shame to pass up that nice reward.

The next morning, accompanied by the officials of the king, Balaam saddled up his faithful donkey and started out for Moab.

As they were going down the road, Balaam's donkey suddenly swerved off into a field. Balaam was furious. He began to beat his donkey and yell at her. Finally, red-faced and sweating, he forced the little beast back onto the road.

The king's officials said nothing, but Balaam could imagine what they were thinking: "*This* is the powerful soothsayer of Pethor? A man who can't even control his own donkey?"

The road to Moab now wound through grape-growing country. There were vineyards on either side of the road, protected by rock walls.

With no warning at all, Balaam's donkey lurched to one side, squeezing Balaam's leg against the rough stones of the wall. Balaam howled out in pain as well as embarrassment. This donkey was making him look like a jackass in front of the king's officials.

Once again he took his stick and beat his little donkey, forcing her back into the center of the road to continue the journey.

Later that day the road narrowed until it was hardly more than a footpath, only wide enough for Balaam and the officials to make their way single file around the side of a hill.

Suddenly, Balaam's donkey plopped down on her stomach, refusing to move a step farther. Balaam had hardly slid off her back before he began to beat the creature unmercifully.

At this, the donkey turned her head toward Balaam and said sadly, "What have I done to make you beat me three times?"

Balaam was so furious, he didn't even stop to wonder that his donkey was talking. "What have you done?" he yelled at her. "Three times you've made me look like a fool in front of the king's officials, that's what! And believe me, if this stick had been a sword, you'd be dead by now."

"You've been riding me for many years," the donkey said. "I've taken you to countless places. Every time your services have been needed, I have faithfully borne you on my back wherever you had to go. Now answer me this: Have I ever before run off the road or slammed into a wall or lain down on the pathway?"

"Well, no," Balaam answered. "You never have before. But that doesn't mean . . ." Just then Balaam looked up. And the sight that greeted his eyes struck him speechless.

"See," said the donkey.

Now Balaam saw what only the donkey had been able to see until then—

the shining creature of Balaam's dream, guarding the narrow passage with
a great flaming sword in his hand.

Balaam threw himself to the road, his nose flat in the dust. He didn't care that the officials of King Balak seemed to see and hear nothing.

He himself was shaking with fright. The angel's robes were so dazzling they blinded his eyes, and the heat from the burning sword scorched his forehead. He did not dare raise his eyes to look at the fearsome messenger again.

"Why have you beaten your poor donkey these three times?" the angel asked Balaam in a voice of thunder.

Balaam was too terrified to reply.

"Could it be that a donkey is wiser than the great soothsayer of Pethor? And more perceptive than the officials of the king of Moab? Was a donkey the only one who could see me standing in the way, trying to prevent you from going to Balak? Surely," the angel continued, "surely you know that this journey is odious in the sight of God."

Lightning flashed in the angel's eyes, but Balaam didn't see, for he still did not dare lift his nose off the ground.

"You foolish man! Your donkey saved your life. Not once, but three times. If she hadn't shied away from me, this sword would have cut you through. Though," and the angel's voice grew gentle, "I would never have harmed her."

"May heaven forgive me," murmured Balaam, his mouth full of dust. "I have done terrible wrong both to the God of Israel and to this beast. I will turn around and go home at once."

"No," said the angel. "Go on to the palace and see the king. But you are to utter only the words that God puts into your mouth."

Balak had heard that his officials were returning and bringing Balaam with them, so he rushed to the border to meet them.

"Balaam! What has taken you so long?" Balak demanded. "Didn't I offer you enough for your services?"

"I have come," said Balaam, "but an angel stopped me on the way. He told me that whatever words the God of the Israelites puts into my mouth, those are the words I must say."

Balak paid no attention to Balaam's warning. He killed sheep and oxen and made a great feast for Balaam and the officials who had brought him to Moab.

The next day the king took Balaam to the heights above the city, from which they could see the Israelite camp. Now Balak would have his curse!

But Balaam looked down at the tents of the Israelites and said, "How can I curse whom God has not cursed? I would die happy if my fortune were as great as the fortunes of these Israelites!"

Balak was furious. "What have you done?" he asked. "I brought you up here to curse the Israelites, and you have blessed them instead."

"I can't help it," Balaam answered. "I can say only what God tells me to say."

So Balak took Balaam to the top of Mount Pisgah, from which he could see another part of the Israelite encampment. Here Balak built seven altars and sacrificed a bull and a ram on each one. Then once again he ordered Balaam to curse the Israelites.

But Balaam would say only the words that God allowed him to say.

"God is not a human being that he should lie, nor a mortal that he should change his mind. God has commanded me to bless, and God has blessed. I can't take back that blessing."

Balak was angrier than ever. "Don't curse them at all, then," he said. "Just don't bless them, either!"

"I can say only what God tells me to say," Balaam answered. "And God will make these people prosper like gardens that grow beside a river. God will exalt their kings and strike down their enemies. Blessed is everyone who blesses them, and cursed is everyone who curses them."

The king clapped his hands together in rage. "What's the matter with you?" he cried. "I sent for you to come and curse my enemies, and you persist in blessing them. Is this how you think you're going to get a reward from me?"

Balaam answered, "I warned your officials. I told them that even if they gave me a house piled with silver and gold I would not disobey the word of the Lord, the God of the Israelites."

"Go home!" the king of Moab shouted. "Leave at once. You and your wretched donkey!"

"Before I go," said Balaam, "I have one more word to deliver:

Behold, a star shall rise out of Jacob, and a scepter shall rise out of Israel.
It shall crush the boundaries of Moab."

Poor Balak. He had sent for Balaam to curse his enemies, only to have his own nation cursed. For whomever Balaam the soothsayer of Pethor blessed was blessed indeed, and whomever he cursed was truly cursed.

With that, Balaam got on his faithful donkey and rode peacefully home to Pethor where, as far as we know, neither Balaam nor his donkey ever saw another angel.

Afterword

In the Hebrew Bible there are only two talking animals. The first is the serpent in the Garden of Eden that tempts Eve to eat the forbidden fruit. The second is the wise donkey who belongs to the heathen soothsayer Balaam. The story of Balaam and his ass is a comic story buried in the Book of Numbers. On either side of the story is the solemn account of Israel's wandering in the wilderness and her entry at last into Canaan.

As you may know, the Bible had many authors and many editors. The story of Balaam's donkey is a good example of how the Bible got put together. A bare-bones account of the story was written down by a writer scholars call J who, it is thought, lived about nine hundred years before Christ, during the reign of King Solomon's son Rehoboam. Rehoboam was a greedy and foolish king, and during his reign the northern part of Israel rebelled and formed a separate kingdom.

J (called "J" because the name of God in the J text is Jahweh or Yahweh) sought to preserve the old, often-told stories from Israel's past. J was a down-to-earth writer who had a good sense of humor. The story of creation in Genesis 2 is primarily J's story. The God described by the priestly writer of Genesis 1 creates by word and by Spirit. In J's account of creation, God is much more like a human being. God shapes man out of clay and breathes into his nostrils the breath of life. J gives us the story of the serpent tempting Eve. In fact, J tells so many stories about women that at least one scholar thinks J may have been a woman [Harold Bloom, *The Book of J*, New York: Grove Weidenfeld, 1990, p. 9].

The stories collected by J were combined by later editors with those from a source called E (in which God is primarily called Elohim); from P, the priestly source (which is concerned with ritual and worship); and from D (the Deuteronomic source, which is largely concerned with religious law). In addition to the J, E, P, and D sources which comprise the first five books of the Bible, the words of other writers, prophets, poets, government scribes, storytellers, kings, and ordinary people were also included in the later books. What were once hundreds of stories, records, and poems became, through the work of many writers and editors over a period of about a thousand years, one unified book which Jews know as the Hebrew Bible and which most Christians call the Old Testament.

The story of Balaam and his donkey is different from most other stories in the Bible because it is told from the viewpoint of persons who were not Israelites or Jews (as the Israelites were later called). But the reason it is included in the Bible is clear. The writers and editors of this story wanted everyone to know that the God of Abraham, Isaac, and Jacob took care of the children of Israel. Even when the people were disobedient or disbelieving, God loved them and led them out of slavery into the land of promise. No heathen soothsayer or enemy king could stand in the way. And the writer J makes both soothsayer and king look like jackasses themselves. If a snake led Eve into disobedience, a donkey would shove Balaam into obedience.

The story as I have retold it leans most heavily on the J account, although the blessings and curses that Balaam delivers probably came from some other writer. You may enjoy comparing the story in this book with the fuller account in the Book of Numbers, beginning with chapter 22 and going through chapter 24. You might also like to note that Balaam's donkey is mentioned in the New Testament as well. The writer of the second letter of Peter compares disobedient people of his own day with Balaam, who "loved the wages of doing wrong, but was rebuked for his own transgression; a speechless donkey spoke with a human voice and restrained the prophet's madness" (2 Peter 2:15–16, NRSV).